JUST GRANDPA AND ME

BY MERCER MAYER

A Paperwing Press™ Book

A GOLDEN BOOK • NEW YORK
Western Publishing Company, Inc., Racine, Wisconsin 53404

My Mom said I need a new suit.

So we went to the city to buy one,
just Grandpa and me.

I bought the train tickets,
but I let Grandpa pay.

I taught Grandpa how to sing "Ninety-nine bottles of pop on the wall."

We went to the big department store.
The revolving door went around and
around and around.

We went around, too,
just Grandpa and me.

I held Grandpa's hand
so he wouldn't get lost.

He did anyway.

Lucky for Grandpa I found him
right away.

CRITTER SUITS →

We took the escalator to the
suit department.
I told Grandpa to hold on tight
to the rail.

Then Grandpa helped me choose
a shirt and tie.

I put on my new suit
and Grandpa said,
"You sure look great!"

Then we went to the movies.
I sat close to Grandpa
in the scary parts
so he wouldn't be afraid.

We had supper in a Chinese restaurant.
I showed Grandpa how to use chopsticks.

Then we got back on the train.
Grandpa took a nap, but not me.
I couldn't wait for Mom
to see my new suit.

We were so proud—
just Grandpa and me.